Hippo Has A Hat

MACMILLAN CHILDREN'S BOOKS

Hippo Has A Hat

Written by
Julia Donaldson

Illustrated by
Nick Sharratt

Lots of clothes! Let's try them.

Maybe we can buy them.

Tiger tries a shirt.

Leopard likes this skirt.

Hippo has a hat.

A cardigan for Cat.

Camel finds a coat.

An anorak for Goat.

Toad's tracksuit is too big.

These jeans are tight on Pig.

Zebra's zip has stuck.

Shoes for Caterpillar.

Slippers for Gorilla.

Flamingo buys a bag.

A string of beads for Stag.

Now everyone looks smart . . .

So let the party start!

For Tom
J.D.

For Henry
N.S.

First published 2006 by Macmillan Children's Books
This edition published 2007 by Macmillan Children's Books
a division of Macmillan Publishers Limited
20 New Wharf Road, London N1 9RR
Basingstoke and Oxford
Associated companies throughout the world
www.panmacmillan.com

ISBN: 978-1-4050-2192-0

Text copyright © Julia Donaldson 2006
Illustrations copyright © Nick Sharratt 2006

11 13 15 17 18 16 14 12

A CIP catalogue record for this book is available from the British Library.

Printed in China